Josie Smith in Winter

D1295662

MAGDALEN NABB

Josie Smith in Winter

Illustrations by Karen Donnelly

Collins
An imprint of HarperCollinsPublishers

First published in Great Britain by Collins in 1999
Collins is an imprint of HarperCollins*Publishers*
77-85 Fulham Palace Road, Hammersmith,
London W6 8JB

The HarperCollins website address is
www.**fire**and**water**.com

1 3 5 7 9 6 4 2

Text copyright © Magdalen Nabb 1999
Illustrations copyright © Karen Donnelly 1999

ISBN 0 00 675407 4

The author and illustrator assert the moral right to be
identified as the author and illustrator of the work

Printed and bound in Great Britain by
Caledonian International Book Manufacturing Ltd,
Glasgow G64

CONTENTS

JOSIE SMITH AND FRIENDS

Josie Smith

Ginger

Mum

Gran

Eileen

Geoffrey Taylor

Gary Grimes

Jimmy Earnshaw

Rawley Baxter

Rawley's sister

Miss Potts

Mr Scowcroft

Mr Kefford

Mrs Chadwick

Ann Lomax

Tahara

JOSIE SMITH IN THE RAIN

Every day it rained. The water swilled down Josie Smith's street and gurgled in the grates and wet the black stones of the houses and crept under the doors to wet the doormats. It splashed and dribbled on the windows and soaked the hoods on the babies' prams.

On Saturday afternoon Josie Smith knelt up on the chair at the front room window and watched the people going past in her street. Not very many of them went past because it was raining and windy and cold.

They all had umbrellas, black or dark green or flowered or scotch plaid, and they walked with their heads down and the umbrellas held in front so the wind couldn't blow the rain in their faces. They all wore raincoats as well and wellingtons and gloves and headscarves and caps and gloves. The people who didn't have umbrellas kept their heads down and their hands in their pockets. They still got wet.

Nearly everybody had flu or a really bad cold and some people had bronchitis. Josie Smith didn't. She used to get tonsillitis but then she had her tonsils out and now she only got colds. She didn't have a cold now, though. She was just fed up.

She had been kneeling up at the window for ages watching for people going past in the rain to get to Mrs Chadwick's shop on the corner opposite. Only two people went past and nobody's umbrella blew inside out. Mrs Scowcroft came past in a green raincoat and a red and black check umbrella in front of her face and went round the corner towards the shops on the main road. When she came back again and went down the street, she held her umbrella behind her head this time so it didn't blow inside out.

Then Mr Scowcroft splashed past in his great big wellingtons. He never had an umbrella. He had a long fawn raincoat on and a cap and a big sack that he held over his head and shoulders. He was going to his allotment to feed his hens. Mr Scowcroft's allotment was just up the road near Josie Smith's school and sometimes he let Josie Smith help him and gave her an egg.

Then Mr Scowcroft was gone and there was nothing to look at except the black street and the rain. Josie Smith pressed her nose to the window and sniffed at the cold glass. She could smell the rain that was whipping and trickling on the outside. It smelled like dirty water.

Josie Smith liked the smell of rain but she liked it best when it smelled of grass. She climbed down from her chair. Josie Smith was fed up with staying in the house. She wanted to go out.

"Mum?"

No answer.

"Mum! I want to play out."

No answer. Josie's mum was lying on the

couch and she had a book in her hand but she
wasn't reading – she was fast asleep and her
face was red. Josie's mum had flu. The doctor
had been to see her and told her to drink a lot
of fluids and rest.

"What's Fluisanress, Mum?" asked Josie
Smith. "Is it like the medicine I used to have
for tonsillitis?"

"No," said Josie's mum. "Now don't pester.
When I've had this lemon tea I'll have to lie
down for an hour."

"And have I to play out and then I won't be pestering you?"

"No," said Josie's mum, "you'll get wet. I don't want you ill as well as me. Find something to do."

Josie Smith was good at finding something to do when it rained. She liked sitting on the hearthrug where it was warm, with Ginger the cat. Ginger was fat and soft and never scratched when she put her arm round him to whisper secrets near his whiskers. She liked cutting out the silver paper saved from chocolate bars to make stars and magic wands and treasure boxes for her pictures. She liked painting and crayoning and reading and writing stories that she made up herself.

But it had rained every day for days and days and days. Ginger had gone out early in the morning and hadn't come back in. When he got caught in the rain he would jump over a wall into somebody's back yard and shelter in their coal shed until it stopped. So she couldn't sit and talk to Ginger. There wasn't a single scrap of silver paper left in her cutting-out box because yesterday she'd made a bridal bouquet with tissue paper flowers and wrapped her last piece of silver paper round it. She couldn't play at weddings by herself. She always played at weddings with Eileen next door. Eileen had a bride doll. She had finished her library book and coloured in the very last picture in her crayoning book.

Perhaps, if she looked out the window again she might see somebody going past. Somebody new she'd never seen before, like a girl who was a real ballet dancer or a nurse in a uniform or a man selling balloons and monkeys on sticks like at the market. If somebody like that went past she could make up a story about them. Josie Smith climbed back on the chair at the window and looked out as hard as she could, feeling excited just thinking of the people she might see.

But the street was dark and rainy and empty.

Josie Smith looked and waited and waited and looked but the street just got darker and rainier and emptier.

Josie Smith leaned her forehead on the cold glass, smelled the dirty rain and then got down again. It was dark in the front room because of the rain and very, very quiet. Even the fire was quiet and a dull dark red. Josie's mum was quiet because she was poorly. It wouldn't be so sad with the light on. But the light would wake Josie's mum up. Josie Smith stood still in the gloomy room in her stockinged feet and she felt so lonely and sad that she wanted to cry. But she didn't cry. She decided something. You can't decide something and cry at the same time.

She tiptoed nearer to the couch.

"Mum…" she said in the tiny voice she used when she wanted to tell her mum something without waking her up properly.

"Mf," said Josie's mum, holding her head tight and frowning in her sleep.

"Have you got a headache, Mum?"

"Mf."

"I'm going out a minute," said Josie Smith in a voice so quiet she could hardly hear it herself.

"Mf," said Josie's mum.

"But I'm only going to Eileen's next door and I'll not get wet."

"Mf," said Josie's mum. Then she opened one eye. "Call at your gran's after," she said, "and ask her to bring us something for tea.

And put your hood up."

"I will," said Josie Smith.

She got the bride's bouquet from her cutting-out box and put it in the pocket of her kilt. Then she went in the kitchen where her wellingtons stood on the mat at the back door. Inside the wellingtons were some extra thick socks. It was cold as well as rainy. Josie Smith pulled on the thick socks and the wellingtons. She put on her dark green anorak with the hood up and its strings pulled tight. She put on one glove because she'd lost the other one and she even put on her itchy scarf which she hated. She looked in the pantry to see if there might be a piece of sacking like Mr Scowcroft wore but there wasn't. She wished she had a piece of sacking. She wished she had an umbrella. Eileen next door had an umbrella, a pink plastic one. Eileen got everything she wanted. She was spoiled, Josie's mum said.

Josie Smith couldn't think of anything else to put on so she pushed the hand with no glove into her anorak pocket, ran to the front door and went out.

The cold rain stung her face but she didn't care. She liked it. She went and knocked at Eileen's door. Eileen opened it.

"Are you playing?" asked Josie Smith.

"No, I'm not," said Eileen, "it's raining. Can't you see? You're daft, you."

"We can play in," said Josie Smith. "I've made a bride's bouquet."

"Well," said Eileen pulling a face, "I don't care because I've got a bride doll and she's got a bouquet and anyway we can't play in because my mum's got flu and I haven't to make a noise."

"Ei-leeeen!" shouted Eileen's mum. "Ei-leeeen! Who is it?"

"It's Josie Smith!" shouted Eileen.

"Tell her to come in a minute!" shouted Eileen's mum.

Josie Smith went in. Eileen's mum was lying on the couch like Josie's mum but the light was on so it wasn't so sad. There was an electric fire as well with pretend flames but Josie Smith didn't like it because you got told off if you threw your toffee papers in it.

"I wish you'd turn that light off," Eileen's mum said, "my head's killing me."

"I'm playing with my doll," said Eileen, "and I want the light on to see."

"Come here, Josie," said Eileen's mum, "I want you to do something for me."

"All right," said Josie Smith.

"Pop back home," said Eileen's mum, "and see if your mum has a packet of aspirin to give me. I've run out."

"My mum's got flu as well," said Josie Smith, "but she takes Fluisanress. I think she's got some aspirin, though."

"Go and see, there's a good girl. Oh dear, it's still pouring down. Have you no umbrella?"

"No, I haven't," said Josie Smith, "but I've got my hood up so it's all right."

Josie Smith went back home to her mum and her mum opened one eye and told her where to find the packet of aspirin in the bathroom.

"Then bring me the packet. You must never touch medicines by yourself."

Josie Smith brought the box and her mum gave her half the aspirins to take to Eileen's mum.

"Tell her that's all I can spare because I'll need these others myself."

"Are they better than Fluisanress?" asked Josie Smith.

"No," said Josie's mum. "They help but fluids and rest are essential. That's what the doctor said." And she lay her poorly head down again.

Josie Smith went back next door and gave the aspirins to Eileen's mum.

"My mum kept a few," said Josie Smith, "but she's taking Fluisanress because the doctor says it's essential."

"Thank you, Josie," said Eileen's mum, "I'll send Eileen's dad to the chemist's for some when he comes in."

"I'm still not playing," Eileen said.

Josie Smith went out. She stood on the doorstep of Eileen's house and the cold rain stung her face but she didn't want to go back home. She ran with her head down to Gary Grimes's house and knocked on the door. Gary Grimes opened the door wearing a thick woolly cardigan with a zip up the front and slippers that had zips up the front too.

"Are you playing out?" asked Josie Smith. Gary Grimes was soft but sometimes he helped her collect worms for Mr Scowcroft's hens.

"I can't play out in this", Gary Grimes said. "I get bronchitis if I get wet. And we can't play in because my mum's got flu."

"Gary!" shouted Gary's mum. "Gary! Who is it?"

"It's Josie Smith!" shouted Gary Grimes.

"Well, tell her to come in a minute!"

Josie Smith went in.

Gary Grimes's mum was lying on the couch like Eileen's mum and Josie's mum. The lamp on top of the television was lit and on the floor by the couch was a little waste basket full of paper handkerchiefs.

Gary's mum opened one eye and said, "I'm not so well, Josie. Do you think your mum would have a box of tissues she could spare me? I've run out and I can't stop sneezing and if our Gary goes out in this weather he'll get bronchitis."

"My mum's got a real handkerchief," said Josie Smith, "and she's got flu and she's taking Fluisanress. It's essential. The doctor said. But Mrs Chadwick sells packets of paper hand-kerchiefs. I've seen them on the counter next to the liquorice torpedoes. I can go and get you some."

"Will you really? That is nice of you. Bring me my bag from that chair."

Josie Smith brought the bag and held out her hand for the money.

"Here you are, that should be enough. That glove's wet, Josie – and where's the other one?"

"I don't know," said Josie Smith. She hoped Gary's mum wouldn't tell her mum because she was always getting shouted at for losing gloves. She ran out of Gary Grimes's front door and the cold rain stung her face but she didn't care. She ran up to Mrs Chadwick's corner shop and went in. The light was on.

"Hello, Josie," Mrs Chadwick said. "What do you want today? Liquorice torpedoes? Sherbet?"

"I haven't come for toffees, I've come for some paper handkerchiefs for Gary Grimes's mum because she's got flu and so has Eileen's mum and my mum has as well".

"My husband's the same," Mrs Chadwick said as she took the money and gave Josie Smith two packets of paper handkerchiefs. "I can't seem to get his temperature down. Is your mum taking anything for it?"

"Fluisanress," said Josie Smith.

"Is she really?" said Mrs Chadwick. "Well if he's no better in the morning I shall have to pop to the chemist's and get some. It's a problem being on my own. I need some fresh eggs from Mr Scowcroft before people start coming in for something for their tea, but I can't go if I've the shop to mind."

"I can go," said Josie Smith. She wanted to go to Mr Scowcroft's to see the hens and sniff the wet grass. She couldn't go just for fun or she'd get shouted at for getting wet. She could go for Mrs Chadwick, though.

"You'll get wet through," Mrs Chadwick

said. "That hood looks wet already. I'll lend you my umbrella."

Mrs Chadwick went in the back and came out with a little green umbrella.

"Is it a little girl's umbrella?" asked Josie Smith.

"No," Mrs Chadwick said. "Come to the door and watch." They went to the door and Mrs Chadwick pushed the umbrella and it grew to the size of a grown-up's umbrella and then it opened.

Josie Smith was pleased. She set off running up to Mr Scowcroft's, her green umbrella bobbing and her wellingtons splashing. The wind tried to blow rain at her from this way and that but Josie Smith kept her umbrella down low, sometimes to the side of her and sometimes to the back, and the rain drummed on it without wetting her.

"Mind it doesn't blow inside out!" shouted

Mrs Chadwick behind her.

But Josie Smith had been watching people go by all day and she knew just what to do. The green umbrella got wetter and wetter and spun round in her hand but it didn't blow inside out. Josie Smith ran faster.

"Don't run back or you'll drop my eggs!" shouted Mrs Chadwick behind her.

Josie Smith knew very well that you don't run when you're carrying eggs but she hadn't got the eggs yet so she ran even faster and jumped in and out of a long puddle – splish-splash-thud.

"Don't...!" shouted Mrs Chadwick behind her, but Josie Smith was too far away and couldn't hear her any more.

When she got to Mr Scowcroft's,
Josie Smith was out of breath.

"Aher! Aher! Aher!" she went, and
she could see her breath in the rain.

"What do you want?" Mr Scowcroft said.
"I haven't time to bother with you." Then he
started coughing.

Josie Smith looked at the wet hens scratching and waited until he'd finished coughing because you shouldn't interrupt people. Then she said, "I've come for Mrs Chadwick's eggs, Mr Scowcroft. Have you got a cough, Mr Scowcroft?"

"Bronchitis," Mr Scowcroft said. He gave her a tray of eggs from his shed. Then he said, "You'll want a bit of sacking over them in this weather." He got a piece of sacking out of the shed and then he said, "You can't hold a tray *and* an umbrella, can you?"

Josie Smith closed the green umbrella. She didn't know how to make it small again so she hooked it on her arm and took the tray of eggs. The piece of folded-up sacking smelled of hen meal and Mr Scowcroft's shed. Josie Smith held on to it with her thumbs. She looked at Mr Scowcroft and waited to see if he would tell her not to run with the eggs but he didn't.

Mr Scowcroft always talked to her the same as he did to grown-ups. His pipe was in his mouth like it always was but there was no smoke coming out of it. Josie Smith went away in the rain and walked very slowly, being careful with the eggs. The wind blew the rain at her and stung her face but it couldn't get at the eggs under their piece of sacking that smelled of hen meal and Mr Scowcroft's shed. Josie Smith's fringe got so wet that the water trickled and tickled down her nose and plopped on to the sacking and made her laugh. She liked being out in the rain. When she got back to Mrs Chadwick's, Mrs Scowcroft was there buying a loaf.

Josie Smith put the tray of eggs on the counter very carefully and took off the piece of sacking. She didn't say anything because they were talking and you shouldn't interrupt.

"He was coughing all night," Mrs Scowcroft

said. "I don't think I closed my eyes once."

"I wonder if Fluisanress would do him any good," Mrs Chadwick said. "I should try him on that if I were you." Then she said, "Thank you very much, Josie. Now go straight home and get dry."

"I've got to go to my gran's," said Josie Smith, "to ask her to bring something for our tea."

Mrs Scowcroft felt Josie Smith's hood.

"She's wet," Mrs Scowcroft said.

"Only a bit," said Josie Smith.

"I suppose you'd better take my umbrella," Mrs Chadwick said, "but mind you bring it back. You know what you are for forgetting things."

"Can I have this sack instead?" asked Josie Smith. "It won't matter, will it, if I forget a sack?" She wanted the sack so she could walk up to the allotment pretending to be Mr Scowcroft.

"If you want," Mrs Chadwick said.

So Josie Smith put the sack over her head and shoulders and ran out of Mrs Chadwick's shop, right down to the bottom of the street and in at her gran's front door.

"Gran!" she shouted, "Gran! You have to come because my mum's got flu and so has Gary Grimes's mum and Eileen's mum as well and my mum says will you bring her something for our tea!"

Nobody answered.

She ran in the kitchen and shouted, "Gran?"

Nobody answered.

She ran in the front room and her gran was there. She was lying on the couch in front of the fire with her hand on her head like Josie's mum and a box of paper handkerchiefs on the floor like Eileen's mum and a cough like Mr Scowcroft's.

"Have you got flu, Gran?" asked Josie Smith.

"I think I must have," said Josie's gran.

"How's your mum?"

"She's poorly," said Josie Smith, "and she said will you bring us something for our tea when you come."

"I can't come today," said Josie's gran, "not now I've got flu. You go in the kitchen and take some ham and lettuce and bread – and take sliced bread. Your mum doesn't like it, but you can't use the breadknife. Then runhome like a good girl and make some sandwiches and lemon and barley water. Can you do that?"

"Yes," said Josie Smith.

"Good girl."

Josie Smith ran up home through the rain as fast as she could go, holding a carrier bag of food in one hand and the sack over her head with the other. She smelled the hen shed smell of the sack and the wet street smell and the smell of things frying for tea coming from all the houses on the way. Her face was wet and her wellies were wet. She was hungry and happy and tired.

When she got home her mum was sitting up. She had poked the fire so it burned more cheerfully and she said she was feeling better.

"Did you get wet?" she asked Josie Smith.

"Only my face and my fringe and one hand…"

"One hand?" repeated Josie's mum. "Have you lost your gloves again?"

"Only a bit," said Josie Smith. "I'm going to make the tea."

Josie Smith made two sandwiches for her mum with ham and mustard and some lettuce. She mixed some lemon and barley water in a glass and took everything to her mum by the fire.

"Thank you very much," said Josie's mum and then she looked at her hard.

"Are you sure you didn't get wet? I don't want you getting ill."

"I'm not ill," said Josie Smith, "and now I'll make my tea."

She made a sandwich with some ham and then looked at the mustard jar. The mustard jar was cut glass with a lid and a tiny, tiny spoon. Josie Smith liked the mustard jar and she liked the bright yellow colour of the mustard. Her mum mixed it up like the powder paint at school but she never let Josie Smith eat it.

"You won't like it," she always said.

But when Josie Smith didn't want to eat something her mum always said, "You don't know whether you like it or not until you've tried it."

Josie Smith looked at the mustard and then at her sandwich and then she had a good think. When she'd finished thinking she said to herself, "I might not like it so I'd better not put it in my sandwich. I'll try it and see whether I like it or not."

The tiny, tiny spoon in the mustard pot was very nice and Josie Smith liked it. But it was really only big enough for feeding your doll or for dotting a bit of mustard on your sandwich when you knew you liked it. It really wasn't big enough for trying things. When you try things you need plenty to make sure. Josie Smith got the biggest spoon that would fit in the pot and took a big scoop of the lovely yellow stuff.

"Like bright yellow ice cream," she said and she smiled and she swallowed it down.

"Aaaaagh!" screamed Josie Smith.

"Whatever's the matter?" called Josie's mum.

"Nothing!" shouted Josie Smith. "Oooh dear." Her lips burned and her tongue burned and her throat burned and her tummy burned. Her eyes watered and she felt sick and she started sweating all over. "I don't think I like it," said Josie Smith, and she ran to the sink and drank some water and washed the spoon because she could hear her mum coming.

"Josie? Josie! Come here."

Josie Smith went. Her mum lifted her chin up to look at her. "Why is your face all red?"

Josie Smith tried to tell her but all she could do was cough.

"You've got a cough!" said Josie's mum, "and you're sweating. You've got a temperature. I told you not to get wet! Go straight to bed and I'll fill you a hot water bottle."

"I don't think I want a hot water bottle," said Josie Smith, "because…"

"Get to bed," said Josie's mum, "and I'll bring you a hot drink."

"I don't think I want a hot drink," said Josie Smith. "I think I want a cold drink because…"

"Get to bed," said Josie's mum, "and I'll bring you your sandwiches up."

"I don't want mustard on them," said Josie Smith, "because…"

"Get to bed," said Josie's mum. "I won't tell you again."

Josie Smith went to bed.

When her mum had been up and gone down again Josie Smith cried for a bit and then she stopped to eat her sandwiches. You can't eat your sandwiches and cry at the same time. When she'd finished her sandwiches she cried a bit more and then she told Percy Panda what had happened. Percy's head was bigger than Josie's head and he was woolly and friendly and fat. Josie Smith liked to sleep cuddled up to Percy but she didn't cuddle up to him tonight.

"I'm too hot Percy," she told him, "and I'll make you hot as well."

So Josie Smith and Percy slept back to back and when Ginger came in, cold and wet from his day out in the rain, he was very pleased to find a hot water bottle in his basket by the bed.

★ ★ ★

"Wake up, Josie," said Josie's mum, "and how are you feeling this morning?"

Josie Smith opened her eyes and the first thing she thought of was mustard. She could still taste it.

"I'm not ill," she told her mum.

"That's for the doctor to say," said her mum, "and that's him knocking now."

"Oh dear," thought Josie Smith. "If he can tell I've been eating mustard, he'll tell my mum."

When the doctor came up Josie Smith kept very quiet. The only thing she said was "aah" when he looked at her throat.

"She's not ill," the doctor said. "Look at those rosy cheeks." He pinched one.

"If you'd seen her last night..." said her mum.

The doctor looked at Josie Smith very hard. He had a frightening beard and although his eyes were smiley, his forehead was creasy.

"Perhaps," he said, "she was only pretending. Perhaps she wanted some of this new medicine like everybody else."

"What new medicine?" asked Josie's mum.

"Something called Fluisanress," said the doctor. "The chemist telephoned me this morning to ask me about it. He'd never heard of it but he said he'd a queue of people a mile long asking for it. I told him I didn't prescribe it so we decided there must be a new doctor going round visiting all my patients. What do you think, Josie?"

Josie Smith kept very quiet. She didn't think she'd done anything wrong except losing her glove and eating the mustard but you can never be sure with grown-ups. The doctor looked at her hard with smiley eyes and a creasy forehead. Josie Smith looked back at him and tried to smile with a creasy

forehead just in case.
The doctor pinched her
nose and said, "Want
to get up?"

"Yes," said Josie Smith.

"I think you should,"
the doctor said. "What
with everybody getting
the flu I might well be
needing my assistant."

Josie Smith kept very
quiet. When the doctor
had gone downstairs she
crept out on to the
landing to listen to what
he said to her mum. She
couldn't hear what he
said but she heard a very
loud laugh and then the
door banged.

When Josie's mum came back up she was laughing too. She sat on the bed and told Josie Smith all about fluids and rest. Then Josie Smith laughed and told her mum all about the mustard and they both laughed. They didn't tell anybody else though, so people didn't stop pestering the chemist until they had all stopped getting flu.

Percy got flu too. Josie Smith kept him in bed for a whole day and offered him lots of pretend lemon and barley water. But because she loved him very much, she gave him a pretend spoonful of Fluisanress, too. Just in case.

Ginger Gets Lost

When it stopped raining it was cold. All day long the sky was grey and all night the wind howled. It howled and whined and moaned and cried down all the chimneys in Josie Smith's street. Josie Smith hated the wind. Every night when she went to bed she stuck her head under the bedclothes and put her fingers in her ears.

One Saturday night the wind was so loud that even with her head under the bedclothes and fingers in her ears, Josie Smith could still hear it.

"Mum!" she shouted. "Mum! Will you come up?"

The stair light went on.

"What's to do now?" Josie's mum shouted from the bottom of the stairs.

"I'm hungry!"

"You can't be. You've only just had your biscuits. Get to sleep."

And the light went off.

Back under the bedclothes went Josie Smith with her fingers in her ears.

The wind howled and whined and moaned and cried round all the chimney pots out there in the dark. Josie Smith squeezed her ears shut as tight as possible but she could still hear it.

"Mum!" she shouted. "Mum! *Please* will you come up?"

The stair light went on.

"What's to do now?"

"I'm thirsty!"

"You are not thirsty. You've just had your cup of milk. You're pestering me just when I want some peace and quiet. Now get to sleep."

And the light went off.

Back under the bedclothes went Josie Smith with her fingers in her ears.

The wind howled and whined and moaned and cried round all the chimney pots out there in the dark.

Under the bedclothes Josie Smith curled up tight with her forehead pressed against her knees and tried her hardest not to be frightened. She sang a little song to herself and that filled her ears up for a bit but when the song stopped the wind got in. She pulled Percy Panda under the bedclothes with her and tried to keep hold of him tight with her elbows so that she could still keep her fingers in her ears. Then she thought that Percy must be frightened, too, so she put her fingers in his ears.

"I can't keep my fingers in your ears, Percy. I can hear the wind and I'm frightened."

She tried holding one hand over one of Percy's ears and one hand over one of her own but then they could both hear and they were both frightened.

"Oh, Percy, what are we going to do?"

Josie Smith started another song but she was too frightened to sing it. Once, her gran had told her that the best thing to do when you're frightened at night is to think about all the things you like best and cheer yourself up. Josie Smith snuggled her face tight against Percy's fat woolly head and tried to think about ballet dancers in shiny toe shoes and about new crayons that smell warm and waxy, all in a line and pointed in their box. Then she thought of new snow with no footprints in it and water paints with all their special colours with fancy names like silk green and crimson lake. But all the time she was thinking of these things, outside in the dark a big witch with glittering eyes was flying nearer and nearer on the howling wind. She was going to get in at the window.

Holding Percy tight, Josie Smith poked her head out just a bit to make sure the witch hadn't got in. The wind howled and whined and moaned and cried and even in the dark

Josie Smith could see the shape of the curtain move just a bit.

"She's coming in the window, Percy! What are we going to do?"

If the witch got in she would rip Percy's fur with her pointed yellow fingernails and his stuffing would come out and he'd die!

"Mum!" shouted Josie Smith, "You've got to come up! You've *got* to! There's a witch!"

This time the light didn't even go on. Josie's mum was really mad now.

"Now that's enough! I won't tell you again. If I have to come up those stairs, you'll be sorry. Now will you get to sleep!"

Josie Smith didn't hear the wind so much when her mum was shouting, and even the witch was flying away as fast as her broomstick would go, because if Josie's mum came up in a temper she'd be sorry too.

Josie Smith and Percy hugged each other and lay there very quiet.

Josie's mum didn't come up.

Somebody else came up instead.

Somebody who could see in the dark because the light still didn't go on.

Somebody cold but very friendly and hoping to get warm.

"Eeow," he said.

"Ginger! Percy, Ginger's come in! Now we'll be all right."

Ginger wasn't frightened of anything. He didn't care if it was dark or if the wind was howling. He could see in the dark and he could howl as loud as any wind himself when he felt like it. Sometimes he played out at night but usually he slept in his basket next to Josie Smith's bed.

"Where are you, Ginger?" asked Josie Smith

and she felt around in the dark near his basket until she found his soft fur and the loud purring in his chest.

"Your fur's cold," said Josie Smith. "If you come on the bed with Percy and me you can get warm and we won't be frightened of the wind."

She knew that Ginger could easily get warm curled up in his basket but he always jumped on the bed when Josie Smith was upset and if she'd been crying he licked the tears off her cheeks.

Ginger jumped on the bed. He sat on the eiderdown on Josie Smith's tummy and purred. Josie Smith felt his nose come near her cheek to sniff for tears and she smiled in the dark and whispered, "I didn't cry, Ginger. I think Percy cried a bit but I didn't."

Ginger settled down again and purred until all three of them fell asleep.

The next day was Sunday and in the afternoon they went to Josie's gran's for tea.

"Put your old blue coat on," said Josie's mum when they were getting ready to go. "It's warmer than your anorak." They got their coats and scarves on. Josie's mum tied a woolly scarf on her head and Josie Smith put her hood up. She put on one brown glove and put her left hand in her pocket so her mum wouldn't notice she'd lost a glove again.

Out in the empty street the freezing wind was still howling around the chimney pots and the sky was grey and sad.

"I wish it would snow," said Josie Smith.

"It's too cold to snow," said Josie's mum.

When they got there Josie's gran was knitting in her armchair by the fire.

"What a wind!" she said. "Shut that door, you're letting the cold in with you. Take your coats off and come and get warm by the fire."

Josie's mum sat down and warmed her hands while Josie Smith stood looking hard at what her gran was knitting. She was always interested in what her gran was knitting. Sometimes it turned out to be something for her. This time though it was something very peculiar. Josie Smith stared and stared. It was something small and striped. There was a red stripe, an orange stripe, a yellow stripe, a green stripe, a blue stripe, an indigo stripe and a violet stripe. In Gran's knitting bag at her feet there were balls of wool in all these different colours. Josie Smith stared and stared and then she said, "Gran! You're knitting a rainbow!"

"I know I am," said Josie's gran. "It's nice, isn't it?" She smoothed it out on her knee.

"But *why* are you knitting a rainbow, Gran?"

"Oh," said Josie's gran, "I just thought I would. I was in the wool shop yesterday and Mary Schofield was selling off all her odds and ends of wool. There was a big basket full of every colour under the sun so I thought I'd pick one of each colour of the rainbow and there you are."

"And did Mary Schofield not want a rainbow herself?" asked Josie Smith.

Josie's mum, warming her hands, laughed at her and said, "You are a comic, Josie. Mary Schofield has a wool shop to sell wool, not to keep it, you know."

"I do know," Josie Smith said, trying so hard to understand that creases came in her forehead. "And I know that's why Mr Bowker at the newsagent's doesn't keep the best toys in his shop for himself."

Even so, if Josie Smith had a shop full of toys she knew she wouldn't sell her favourite ones to other people. She'd keep the whole drawer full of crayoning books for a start.

"I'll go and put the kettle on, shall I?" said Josie's mum.

"That'd be nice," said Josie's gran.

When Josie's mum was in the kitchen Josie's gran whispered in Josie Smith's ear.

"This rainbow," she said, "just might – you never know – turn into a little pair of mittens."

Josie Smith smiled. "For me?" she whispered.

"If they're your size," said Josie's gran. "We shall have to see. You never know with knitting."

"I know you don't," said Josie Smith. She knew because once her gran had given her some big wooden needles and a ball of thick wool. Josie Smith had knitted as hard as she could to make it turn into a scarf. She had made creases in her forehead and stuck her tongue out and sometimes she even stopped breathing, but the stitches her gran had cast on for her didn't grow into a scarf. Josie Smith poked and looped and turned and pulled and poked and looped and turned and pulled for a whole afternoon. But at teatime there were just the two wooden needles and a long trail of wiggly wool between them with a knot in it. You never know with knitting.

"I hope it does turn into some mittens for me," Josie Smith said.

"Have you still not found your brown glove?"

Josie Smith shook her head. "I'd rather have rainbow mittens really," she said, "than find my brown glove."

"Well," said Josie's gran, "you keep looking, anyway, and I'll keep knitting. And if it turns out there's enough wool maybe I could make a rainbow scarf to match."

Josie's mum came in from the kitchen and set the butter dish on the edge of the hearth to warm. She was going to make the tea because Gran was still getting better from the flu.

When Josie Smith went in the kitchen to help her mum it was lovely and warm because the oven had been on to bake cakes. Even though Josie's gran was still getting better from the flu, she had made Josie's favourite buns with white icing on top. There was a great big plateful of them on the table.

"Don't touch," said Josie's mum.

Josie Smith didn't touch but she wanted to. The soft white icing had dribbled down from the edges of the buns and made icing blobs on the plate. If you were careful you could catch them on your finger and suck them without disturbing the buns.

"Can I just touch… "

"Wash your hands," said Josie's mum, "while I put the cloth on in the other room. Then you can help me set the table."

They drew the thick curtains and switched the light on and poked the fire to make it blaze and then they sat down and had a very good tea. Josie Smith ate so many buns that her tummy was full enough to pop the buttons off her cardigan. When it was time to go back up the dark windy street she had a little paper bag with more buns in it to take home.

"Do you think Ginger likes buns?" asked Josie Smith when they got home.

"No," said Josie's mum. "Put your slippers on."

"I bet he'd lick a bit of icing off my finger," said Josie Smith.

"Ginger's got his own dinner," said Josie's mum and she put some out for him on a saucer.

Josie Smith put her slippers on and then she opened the back door to shout.

"Ginger! Ginger!" But Ginger didn't come in. He wasn't in the back yard.

"I wonder if Percy likes buns," said Josie Smith.

"You can ask him," said Josie's mum. It's bedtime. Get your pyjamas on."

Before she went upstairs to bed Josie Smith opened the front door to shout.

"Ginger!" she shouted. "Ginger!" But Ginger didn't come in. He wasn't on the doorstep.

"Mum," said Josie Smith, "why doesn't Ginger come in for his dinner? He always comes."

"He comes in when we're having our tea," said Josie's mum, "because he sees the light and hears us. But today we were at your gran's. I expect he waited a bit and then went away again. He'll come back now the light's on."

Josie Smith went upstairs and got ready for bed. Then she knelt on her bedroom windowsill and looked out at the dark and windy night. The moon was shining and sometimes a long cloud raced in front of it. In the moonlight Josie Smith could see the shiny slates of all the roofs and the pointy tops of all the chimneys but she couldn't see Ginger. He wasn't on the coal shed roof or on the wall by the gate. The freezing wind howled and whined and moaned and cried around the chimneys in the dark street. Josie Smith shivered and got in bed to hide under the covers with Percy. She lay very still, close to Percy with her fingers in her ears. Then she began to think. She thought about having her tea, cosy and warm in her gran's front room. Then she thought about Ginger out in the freezing cold looking in at the dark kitchen, waiting. She thought about all the good things she'd eaten and her tummy filled to bursting with buns. Then she thought of Ginger waiting for his dinner in the dark and going away hungry and sad.

Josie Smith jumped out of bed crying and knelt on the windowsill again. She pressed her forehead against the cold glass.

"Ginger! Please come home, Ginger! Please!"

The wind howled and whined and moaned and cried round the chimneys in the dark street but Ginger didn't come.

Josie's mum had said that Ginger would come in when he saw the light. Josie Smith looked down in the yard but there was no light from the window. The curtains were closed. Josie Smith got down from the windowsill and ran to the top of the stairs.

"Mum!" she shouted, "Mum! Mum!"

The stair light went on.

"What's to do?" shouted Josie's mum.

"Mum, the curtains are drawn and Ginger won't see the light and he'll think we're still at my gran's and he'll go away again!"

"Are you crying?" asked Josie's mum.

"No," said Josie Smith, but she said it with her eyes shut because it was a lie.

"Well, you get back in bed. Ginger will come

in when he wants to."

"But *please* will you
open the curtains so he
can see you? Mum,
please will you?"

"All right. But you get to
sleep. It's school in the morning."

The stair light went off.

Josie Smith ran back to the windowsill and
saw the light shine out in the yard as her mum
opened the curtains.

"Ginger! You can come now. Ginger! The
light's on and my mum's there and she'll give
you your dinner!"

The wind howled and moaned and whined
and cried around the chimneys in the dark street
but Ginger didn't come.

Josie Smith was frightened of the wind and
the dark night outside but she couldn't go to bed
until Ginger came so she got Percy out of bed

and they waited on the windowsill together. The freezing wind crept in at the cracks round the glass to make Josie Smith shiver so she wrapped the curtain round herself and Percy and waited.

Ginger didn't come.

Josie Smith started counting out loud so she wouldn't hear the wind so much. She counted up to a hundred but Ginger didn't come.

She started counting another hundred. One, two, three, four, five…

Something went bump and Josie Smith opened her eyes.

"I must have fallen asleep," she said. Percy had fallen on the floor. That was Percy going bump. Josie Smith picked him up and looked out of the window. The wind was still howling but the moon had gone away and the light from the kitchen window had gone too. Josie's mum had gone to bed.

Josie Smith looked in Ginger's basket but

Ginger wasn't there. She looked as hard as she could out at the dark night but Ginger wasn't there. The wind howled and whined and moaned and cried round the chimneys and a big lump came in Josie Smith's throat to make her cry. Then she heard something that wasn't the wind. She thought she heard it. Did she hear it? She listened harder. She heard the wind that howled and moaned and whined and cried and then a tiny noise from a long way away went:

"Eeyow, eeyow, eeyow..."

Ginger! It was Ginger's voice but Ginger didn't come.

The wind howled louder and whined and moaned and then:

"Eeyow, eeyow, eeyow..."

Why didn't he come home? Why was he crying? Why was he so far away? Perhaps he'd hurt himself. Perhaps he'd been run over and he couldn't walk.

"Eeyow, eeyow, eeyow…"

Josie Smith ran to the top of the stairs and then into her mum's bedroom to tug at the bedclothes.

"Mum! Mum! I can hear Ginger out in the dark! Mum!"

Josie's mum was fast asleep but she felt Josie's hand touch her face and said in a dozy voice: "You're frozen. What are you doing out of bed? Have you been having a nightmare? Get in with me and I'll warm you."

She lifted up the covers to let her get in and

Josie Smith felt how warm as toast it was in the big bed and how icy cold she was herself but she couldn't get in.

"Mum, I can hear Ginger. He's outside crying."

"It's only the wind," said Josie's mum, and her eyes were still shut fast.

"It's not the wind!" shouted Josie Smith. "I can hear the wind and I can hear Ginger as well and perhaps he's been run over and he's lying in the road crying in the dark! Mum! Please wake up! *Please!*"

Josie's mum stretched out her hand and switched on the bedside light. When she saw Josie Smith's white face and her tears, she opened her eyes wide and sat up to get hold of her.

"Josie! You're shaking all over! Whatever's the matter?" She tried to pull Josie into the snug bed and cover her up with warm bedclothes and love her better but Josie fought her.

"We've got to save Ginger. You've got to come in my bedroom and you'll hear him crying. Quick, Mum!"

When Josie Smith pestered or acted soft or made up witches, her mum didn't come, but now she came. She put on her dressing gown and slippers and let Josie Smith pull her by the hand to the back bedroom window.

"Listen!" she said.

The wind howled and whined and moaned and cried round all the chimneys in the dark street.

"You see," said her mum, "it's the wind."

"Hush, Mum!" said Josie Smith, "and listen."

Josie's mum hushed and listened.

The wind howled and whined and moaned and cried around the chimneys and then:

"Eeyow, eeyow, eeyow!" went Ginger.

"You see," said Josie Smith, "that's Ginger."

"I heard him," said Josie's mum. "That's Ginger all right. Get your clothes on. Be quick."

Josie Smith put all her clothes on over her pyjamas because she thought that was the quickest way, but when she ran downstairs she saw that her mum had been even quicker. She had her coat and scarf on and she was looking in the top drawer in the kitchen for the torch she used when the lights fused.

"Thank goodness for that," said Josie's mum. "The battery's a bit weak but it's working. Get your coat on. Wrap up well."

And when Josie Smith had wrapped up well they went out the back gate into the night and the howling wind. They turned the corner and

went down between the backs of the houses.

"How do you know it's this way?" whispered Josie Smith.

"Because you heard him from the back bedroom. Look in all the gateways. You're not frightened, are you?"

"No," said Josie Smith with her eyes shut tight. She felt a bit frightened but she felt much more worried about Ginger so she didn't care. She held her mum's hand and looked in all the dark gateways where her mum pointed the torch. Sometimes there were beetles and once a mouse that jumped out and ran away. Halfway down the back somebody had forgotten to take their

washing in and they had to push through some trouser legs and sheets that flapped in the howling wind and hit them hard in the face.

"Ginger…" whispered Josie Smith. "Ginger, where are you?"

"Louder," said Josie's mum. "He'll recognise your voice and answer."

"Ginger! Ginger!" shouted Josie Smith. It seemed very strange to be shouting in the middle of the night. "Ginger! Ginger!"

"Eeyow, eeyow, eeyow!"

"He's here! Mum, he's here in this gateway."

And there he was. Hunched up, cold and miserable with his fur sticking up and his white chest and paws all dark and dirty.

Josie Smith bent down to pick him up.

"No," said Josie's mum, "don't touch him. He must be hurt and if you try and pick him up you could hurt him more."

"What's happened to him?" asked Josie Smith.

"We'll soon see," said Josie's mum. "Hold the torch so I can see him."

Josie Smith held the torch and Josie's mum bent down and felt Ginger very carefully from his head all the way to his tail. Then she felt his legs and paws.

"Shsht!" spat Ginger because that was his way of saying "ouch".

"Ah…" said Josie's mum.

"What's happened to him?" asked Josie Smith. "Has he been run over?"

"No," said Josie's mum. "He's trodden on

some glass and it's stuck in his paw so he can't walk. He'll be all right. Let's get him home."

"Can I carry him?" asked Josie Smith.

"No," said Josie's mum. "He's very heavy for you and you could hurt him by accident. You carry the torch and hold that washing aside so it doesn't touch him."

When Josie's mum picked him up very carefully, Ginger began to purr.

"Listen to him," said Josie Smith. "Why is he happy when he's still got glass in his paw?"

"He's happy because we've found him," said Josie's mum. "If it hadn't been for you he'd have been out all night by himself, cold and hungry and in pain."

They took Ginger home and in the kitchen Josie's mum pulled out the piece of glass with her tweezers. Then she washed the blood off his paw and put disinfectant on it like she did when Josie Smith fell.

"He can't have a plaster on, though, can he, Mum? Because of his fur."

"No," said Josie's mum. "I'll put him a bandage on for a day or two and then after that it will heal better in the air and he'll keep it licked clean himself."

"Mum, why has he got blood on his white chest as well?"

"I really don't know." Josie's mum washed Ginger's chin and chest and looked under his fur but there were no cuts.

Then they gave Ginger his saucer of food.

"Eeyow," said Ginger, going close and sniffing it. "Eeyow." But he didn't eat it.

"It's your favourite dinner, Ginger," said Josie Smith, pushing it nearer.

"Eeyow," said Ginger but he didn't eat it.

"Just a minute," said Josie's mum and she picked Ginger up and sat him on her knee. Then she pushed her little finger in the side of his mouth and he opened it and showed her his tongue.

"Oh, poor Ginger," said Josie's mum, "he must have tried to lick his paw better and he's cut his tongue on the glass. That's why there was blood on his chin and chest. He won't be able to eat properly for a while."

"But he has to eat something," said Josie Smith, "or he'll die."

"He has to drink something, that's more important. He won't die."

Josie's mum went in the pantry and searched for a long time in the cupboards until she found a feeding bottle.

"This was yours when you were a baby," she said. "You used to drink orange juice from it."

"But Ginger didn't have orange juice from a bottle," said Josie Smith. "He won't know how to do it."

"He had milk from his mum. He won't be able to suck with his sore tongue but I'll drop the

milk into the
side of his mouth. He'll
manage." Ginger managed.

"Now, you two," said Josie's mum. "Do you
know what time it is? It's three o'clock in the
morning and here we are with our coats on.
What about going to bed?"

So they went to bed. They were so cold that
they all slept together in Josie's mum's bedroom.
Ginger lay on the eiderdown with his bandaged
paw in the air and purred. Josie Smith cuddled
up to her mum and in between you could just
see, sticking out from the bedclothes, Percy's
woolly ears.

When Josie Smith woke up, she opened her
eyes and her mum was looking down at her. The

radio was playing music downstairs and out in the street people were sweeping and shaking doormats and talking. The wind was blowing but not so hard and there were some dinner smells.

Josie Smith opened her eyes wider.

"Am I late for school?" she said.

"You're not going to school – at least not until after dinner. I popped up and explained to Miss Valentine. Get washed and dressed now."

"Where's Ginger gone?" asked Josie Smith.

"He's downstairs on the rug by the fire looking very important with his bandage."

"Will he be able to eat his dinner today?" asked Josie Smith.

"He has eaten it," said Josie's mum. "Eileen's mum lent me her liquidizer and I put some liver through it so I could get it in his mouth through a big hole in your feeding bottle. He can't lap yet but he liked it."

Josie Smith smiled. Then she stopped smiling and sniffed at the dinner smells with a very worried look on her face.

"I'm not having liver, am I?"

"No," said Josie's mum, "you're having a nice little chop and some mashed potatoes and sprouts."

Josie Smith smiled again. She got up and dressed.

Everybody in the street had heard about Ginger's accident and some people sent presents. Mr Scowcroft sent a speckled egg for Josie Smith to build her strength up after being up half the night. Mrs Chadwick sent Ginger a tin of his favourite cat food for when he could eat properly again and Eileen bought him a clockwork mouse from Mr Bowker's newsagent's and toyshop because he couldn't play out.

The day that Ginger's paw was better and he could play out, Josie Smith went out to play too.

It wasn't so cold any more.

She ran up to Mr Scowcroft's allotment to say thank you for the speckled egg.

"Ginger's better now, Mr Scowcroft," she said.

"Aye," Mr Scowcroft said. He always said aye instead of yes and when Josie Smith asked him why he didn't tell her. Mr Scowcroft was standing in the middle of his allotment looking up at the sky with his pipe in his mouth. It didn't have smoke coming out of it, though, because Mr Scowcroft still had a bit of bronchitis. The hens climbed over his big wellingtons and pecked at the hard ground looking for worms.

"Shall I help you feed the hens, Mr Scowcroft?" asked Josie Smith.

"Aye," Mr Scowcroft said.

When they were feeding the hens, Josie Smith

said, "Ginger had blood all over his fur and he couldn't eat his dinner and I thought he was going to die."

"If a cat," said Mr Scowcroft, "broke its leg and one half of the leg was over there," he pointed his pipe at the cabbages, "and the other half was over here," he pointed it at the hen shed, "the two halves of that leg would shuffle towards each other and stick themselves back together and back on to that cat. You don't want to be worrying about cats. Cats have nine lives."

"What does that mean, Mr Scowcroft?" asked Josie Smith.

But Mr Scowcroft didn't answer. Mr Scowcroft only said things because he wanted to say them, not because you asked him things. He finished feeding the hens and then he took an egg from his pocket and gave it to Josie Smith.

"Thank you, Mr Scowcroft. Have I to go now, Mr Scowcroft?"

Mr Scowcroft stood very still looking up at the sky and made a whistling noise through his pipe.

"It's going to snow," he said at last, and he went inside his shed.

Josie Smith looked up at the sky like Mr Scowcroft did. It looked soft and grey and quiet. She couldn't see any snow but Mr Scowcroft always knew about the weather.

"It's going to snow," she whispered. "It's going to snow."

Then she ran home as fast as she could to tell the good news to Ginger.

Josie Smith in the Snow

After tea, Josie Smith helped to clear the table in the kitchen and then she spread some newspapers on it and got some drawing paper and a jam jar of water and her paintbox. Josie's mum settled down in her chair with the paper and Josie Smith started a picture.

"Mum," she said, "d'you know what? I'm going to paint a snow scene."

"That's nice," said Josie's mum.

Josie Smith made some creases in her

forehead, stuck the tip of her tongue out at the corner of her mouth and started. First she drew. She started drawing her own house first, then she was going to draw all the other houses just the same in a long line. After that she was going to draw all the other streets behind it with their chimneys with pointy tops. Then, behind the houses, the big hill with a tower on top.

"Mum," said Josie Smith, "d'you know what? I'm painting Holcombe Hill and the tower, and near the bottom, in Tag Wood where it's not so steep and you can sledge, I'm going to paint children sledging."

"That's nice," said Josie's mum.

Grown-ups say "That's nice" like that when they're not taking any notice. And when they're not taking any notice, because they're talking or reading the paper or getting ready, you can get on with things and they don't interrupt you. If you don't pester you can even stay up late and they still don't notice. But Josie Smith had to pester a minute.

"Mum," she said, "I want to open the curtains so I can see out in case it starts snowing."

"You can't," said Josie's mum, "because it's dark and cold and it'll be draughty."

"But, Mum!" said Josie Smith, "it's going to snow, Mr Scowcroft said!"

"Well, peep out every so often."

"I want to watch while I'm painting. Can I just open them a tiny bit? Go on, Mum, please."

"Oh, all right, but only a little bit."

Josie Smith opened the curtains just a bit so that she could see out into the yard. She was pleased about that but she had pestered and now her mum was taking notice.

"You can't paint all those things tonight," she said. "You'll have to draw tonight and paint tomorrow."

Josie Smith didn't say "Oh, Mum!" She just

drew. Every now and then she looked out through the gap in the curtains. She drew her own house with the door and the window and the doorstep with Ginger sitting on it. Then she drew Eileen's house next door. There was no cat on the doorstep there but Eileen's baby brother was parked in his pram outside and there was a vase of plastic flowers in the window. Josie Smith stopped drawing and looked out. There were no snowflakes in the dark yard.

Josie Smith started drawing again. Then she stopped.

"Mum," she said, forgetting not to pester, "I want to put Gary Grimes's house in and Rawley Baxter's and Jimmy Earnshaw's and Geoffrey Taylor's but they live on the other side of the street so you can't see them in my picture."

"Put their houses on our side, then," said Josie's mum.

"Can I?" asked Josie Smith. "Is it all right?"

"Of course it's all right", said Josie's mum. "It's your picture and you can draw it however you like."

So Josie Smith drew Gary Grimes standing at the door in his slippers with zips up the front. Then she drew Rawley Baxter's house with Rawley Baxter flying his plastic Batman in the window.

Then she stopped drawing and looked out. There were no snowflakes in the dark yard.

Josie Smith drew. She drew Jimmy Earnshaw's house with his cat Betsy coming out of the door. Betsy was Ginger's mum and she was going to come up the street to see him. Then she drew

Geoffrey Taylor's house with his two-wheeler bike leaning on the wall outside. Geoffrey Taylor's two-wheeler had stabilizers and sometimes he let Josie Smith have a go on it by herself. Jimmy Earnshaw had a two-wheeler bike as well. Sometimes he let Josie Smith have a go on it but there were no stabilizers so he had to hold her on. Jimmy Earnshaw was big and didn't need stabilizers.

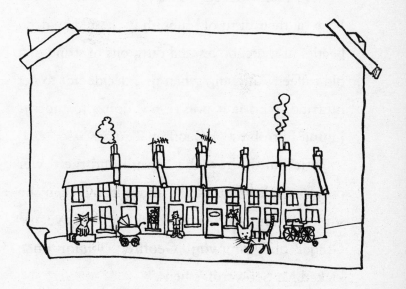

"That *is* nice," said Josie's mum and she said it in a different way now because she was taking notice. She was standing behind Josie Smith looking at the picture and she said, "Have you decided who're you're going to marry between Jimmy Earnshaw and Geoffrey Taylor?"

"I'm not marrying anybody," Josie Smith said, "because you have to kiss them and boys smell horrible. Why do they smell horrible, Mum?"

"It's their pockets," said Josie's mum. "They keep all their dirty old rubbish in them, like dead beetles in matchboxes and dirty bits of string and old toffees. Anyway, when you decide not to get married, who is it you're not going to marry? Jimmy Earnshaw or Geoffrey Taylor?"

Josie Smith drew the big hill and the tower on top while she thought about it and then she said, "Jimmy Earnshaw because he gave me Ginger and, anyway, Geoffrey Taylor once kicked Mr Scowcroft's hens."

"He takes you fishing, though," said Josie's mum.

"His dad takes us," said Josie Smith. "I wish I had a dad. I'd rather have a dad instead of getting married and, anyway, Geoffrey Taylor's got stabilizers. Jimmy Earnshaw's got a real two-wheeler."

"That's settled that, then," said Josie's mum, "and now put all this stuff away and get to bed."

"But I want to wait for the snow," said Josie Smith. "Please let me. Go on!"

"Stop pestering for a minute," said Josie's mum, "and look out the window." She drew the curtains right back.

Out in the dark yard a few big snowflakes were falling. They came down very slowly, twirling about in the air as if they weren't sure of the way down.

"Oooh," whispered Josie Smith, "Mum, look…"

They both looked. The snowflakes began to fall thicker and faster as though now they were all together they didn't need to wander around looking for the way down to the dark ground.

"Mum, there are hundreds and thousands and millions of them! It makes you dizzy. But Mum, where do they disappear to? Why is the yard not all white?"

"It's not sticking," said Josie's mum, "not yet."

"But when will it stick?" asked Josie Smith.

"If it snows all night," said Josie's mum, "it'll stick. You wait and see. Now, bed. The sooner you get to sleep the sooner morning will come. Clear this table."

Josie Smith cleared the table and went to bed as fast as she could so that it would soon be morning. When the light was out and Ginger was curled up in his basket, Josie Smith snuggled up to Percy Panda and told him some secrets.

"Percy, I wish I had a sledge because

sledging's better than snowballing or sliding, and I'm going to build a snowman in the yard for Ginger to sit next to while I'm at school. Oh, Percy, I hope there's loads and loads of snow." She stuck her head out from under the covers but although she listened as hard as she could there wasn't a sound.

"Shh, Percy, don't breathe."

Still not a sound.

"Shh, Ginger, don't purr. So many snowflakes *must* make a little tiny noise."

But there was no little tiny noise. There was no noise at all. It was so very quiet that Josie Smith and Ginger fell fast asleep. Only Percy Panda's eyes stayed open. Pandas know a lot about snow and Josie Smith says that when nobody's watching him, Percy moves. So perhaps that night he was lying awake, watching and waiting for the snow.

"Josie! Josie! Wake up and look out of your window!"

Josie Smith got out of bed so fast that she was still asleep and she nearly put her foot in Ginger's basket. Ginger just opened one eye, stretched himself out and curled himself up and went straight back to sleep.

Josie Smith pulled the curtains back and sat down on the windowsill. She remembered that there was something exciting to look for and that's what had made her jump out of bed. She couldn't remember exactly what it was because she was still so sleepy that her eyes wouldn't stay open. It wasn't Christmas because Christmas had gone past. So, what was it? Josie Smith tried as hard as she could to wake up properly but the more she tried to open her eyes wide the more they wanted to squeeze themselves shut and everything looked funny. She blinked and stared and stared and blinked but she couldn't understand it at all. She rubbed at the cold glass with her warm fist and blinked even harder, trying to remember. First she remembered snow, then she remembered her picture of a snow scene. Then she woke up properly.

"Mum!" she shouted. "The snow's stuck, Mum!"

She stared and stared out of the window. She was wide awake now but everything looked funny just the same and some things weren't there at all. She could see some black chimneys and then behind those some grey chimneys and behind those some chimneys that were so pale and grey they were like ghosts of chimneys and behind those there were no chimneys at all where there should have been lots. There was nothing. And up behind that, where the hill with a tower should be, there was more nothing and up above that there was nothing instead of the sky.

Josie Smith looked down in the yard where

the snow had stuck and she saw part of a brush sticking up and part of a bucket lying down. But snow should be shining white and sparkling blue. This snow had no colour at all. It was pale and sad like the empty sky and the space where the hill and the tower should be. No matter how hard Josie Smith blinked she couldn't see anything properly. The whole world was empty and quiet and grey.

"You see?" said Josie's mum. "I told you it would stick." She put Percy on the windowsill with Josie Smith and started pulling the sheets off the bed.

Josie Smith was thinking hard with creases in her forehead.

"Mum," she said when she'd finished thinking. "D'you know what?"

"What?" said Josie's mum.

"It's only a drawing," said Josie Smith.

"What's only a drawing?" said Josie's mum.

"The snow," said Josie Smith. "It's only a drawing and the drawing's not finished. There should be more chimneys and Holcombe Hill's not in it and the tower. And none of it's been painted in yet. Look."

Josie's mum looked out of the window and laughed.

"Well," she said, "you haven't painted yours in either, have you? Don't worry. It just means there's still a lot of snow that has to fall. Then the sun will come out and everything will be coloured in and the snow will sparkle. Now, change Ginger's sheet and get ready for school or you'll be late."

Ginger's basket had wool stuffing from an old pillow in it to make it snug. Over the wool there was an old tea-towel for a sheet. When Josie's mum changed Josie's sheets, Josie Smith changed Ginger's. When she was dressed she took his dirty sheet down and washed it in a bowl in the kitchen.

"I can't put it out to dry, can I?" she said.

"No," said Josie's mum, "it's going to snow again. Squeeze it out and leave it there and come and have your breakfast."

After breakfast Eileen next door came and rattled at the letter box. Josie Smith was fastening her coat up.

"Put your scarf on," said Josie's mum. "Have you got your gloves?"

"Yes," said Josie Smith but she said it with her eyes shut because there was only one brown glove in her green anorak pocket. She put on one glove and her itchy green scarf and ran to the door.

"Bye, Mum!" she shouted.

"Tie that scarf!" shouted Josie's mum, but she didn't see the one glove because Josie Smith kept her right hand in her pocket.

Josie Smith and Eileen walked up the road to school. Gary Grimes and Rawley Baxter ran past them kicking up the soft snow in their faces.

"I'm telling over you!" shouted Eileen. "And if you throw snowballs at us I'll tell Miss Potts and then you've had it!"

"You're soft, you!" Rawley Baxter shouted.

"Tell-tale-tit!" Gary Grimes shouted. Then they ran away.

"You shouldn't tell over people," Josie Smith said.

"I don't care," Eileen said, "I'm telling if I want and, anyway, I'm having a sledge. My mum's buying it me this afternoon."

"A real sledge of your own?" Josie Smith's chest went Bam Bam Bam. "Will you let me have a go on it?"

"I might do," Eileen said, "after school. But only if you play what I want to play all day."

"All right," said Josie Smith. They were going past Mr Scowcroft's allotment. "Wait," said Josie Smith, "I have to say Hello to the hens."

"That's stupid," Eileen said.

"It is not," Josie Smith said, "because they're my friends."

"Hens can't be your friends," said Eileen, "and, anyway, you've got to do what I say or you're not having a go on my sledge and I say we've got to go straight to school."

They went straight to school.

It was a horrible morning. They had to do sums and Josie Smith couldn't do them. Sums are like knitting. You try and try and try and all you get is a muddle. Eileen couldn't do them either but she didn't care. She just copied them out and then tidied her pencil case and told everybody she was going to have a new sledge. Ann Lomax and Tahara asked her if they could have a go on it and Eileen said they could. Ann Lomax gave her a full tube of toffees and Tahara gave her a bangle. Josie Smith's chest went Bam Bam Bam because if everybody wanted a go on Eileen's sledge there might not be time for her to have a go. She had no toffees and no bangle to give.

Even playtime was horrible because it had started snowing again and Miss Potts, the headmistress, came round to everybody's classroom and said they couldn't play out. What was the use of snow if you couldn't play out in it? They stayed in their classroom to play. More and more people asked Eileen for a go on her sledge and Josie Smith got more and more worried. After play, when everybody else was reading, Miss Valentine made Josie Smith do all her sums again because she hadn't got a single one right. Outside the big window it snowed and snowed, but the sky was grey and the snow was grey and they had to switch the lights on to see their books. The classroom was too hot and there was a smell of fish and Josie Smith was fed up.

Dinner was fish fingers and peas and horrible little dry chips and Miss Potts blew her whistle and shouted at everybody for making a noise and flicking peas on the floor and standing on them. Then she said they couldn't play out all day because the weather was too bad. The classroom got hotter and hotter and smellier and smellier and Eileen made everybody who wanted a go on her sledge play Simon Says. Rawley Baxter said it was a stupid game but he had a sledge of his own. Josie Smith thought it was a stupid game, too, but she played. At hometime Mr Scowcroft's hens stopped scratching in the soft snow when they saw Josie Smith coming, in case she was going to give them some dinner. Their backs and wings were covered with snowflakes so they had to shake and ruffle themselves. They made little crowing noises but Josie Smith only looked at them as Eileen linked arms and pulled her past the fence.

"What's the matter with you?" said Josie's mum when Josie Smith got home.

"I'm fed up," said Josie Smith, "and I'm hungry and thirsty, as well."

"Take those wellingtons off," said Josie's mum, "and put your slippers on and wash your hands and face and set the table. I've just got to finish this seam."

Josie's mum made frocks for everybody else's mum and sometimes she made them for Josie Smith. When she made wedding frocks and frocks for Christmas dances Josie Smith collected scraps of net and lace for her doll. When she'd put her slippers on she looked at what her mum was pushing through the sewing machine but it was something thick and lumpy that was as grey as the afternoon sky and the sad snow.

"Mum, I'm fed up," said Josie Smith. She was fed up enough to cry.

"Wash your hands," said Josie's mum.

"You're hungry, that's what's wrong. Did you not eat your dinner?"

"I didn't like it," said Josie Smith, "but, Mum, Eileen's having a new sledge and she said I could have a go after school, only now she says everybody can have a go and there won't be time."

"Eileen's not going sledging today," said Josie's mum. "It'll be dark in two minutes and it's still snowing hard. Wash your hands."

Josie Smith washed her hands at the kitchen sink. She sniffed a bit because she still felt like crying. Then she sniffed again.

"Cheese savoury!" she shouted.

"That's right," said her mum.

"And will you do a crispy top on it?" said Josie Smith.

"I always do a crispy top on it," said Josie's mum.

"And baked beans with it?"

"And baked beans," said her mum. "Now,

are you still fed up?"

"No," said Josie Smith, "and after tea I can finish my picture."

So after tea she painted while her mum settled down in her chair to hem the grey wool skirt.

Josie Smith's paint box had tiny squares of colour, each with its name written underneath. Josie Smith liked the names almost as much as she liked the colours. The best names were Scarlet Lake and Crimson Lake and Leaf Green and Silk Green and Chrome Yellow and Indigo. They were very special names. Some of them were so special that you couldn't tell what colour they were at all if you didn't look, like Burnt Umber and Raw Sienna. Sometimes Josie Smith thought about asking her mum what the names meant but she never did because she liked them to be secret. She sometimes said the names to herself in her head but she didn't tell anybody about them. She had to ask her mum something now, though, because she didn't know what to do.

"Mum?"

"Mm?"

"I don't know what to do. I've got a square of white paint but I can't paint the snow with it."

"Why's that?"

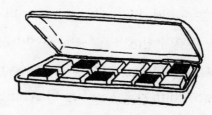

"Because the paper's white so when I put white paint on it I can't see it."

"You don't need it then, do you? Your paper's white so that's the snow and you can just paint the things that haven't got snow on them."

"Like Eileen and Eileen's sledge?"

"That's right. And Ginger."

"Ginger might have a bit of snow on him. Mr Scowcroft's hens did."

"Well, you'll have to be very careful with things that have a bit of snow on them and only paint the parts that haven't."

"All right," said Josie Smith, "but I'm making the winter sun come out so you can see everything and the snow will sparkle." She swished her brush in the clean water, stuck out her tongue and started. It took a long time and Josie Smith got very tired because it got past her bedtime and her mum let her finish. She didn't even clear the table because her painting had to be left out to dry.

"Just wash your brushes," said Josie's mum, "and I'll see to everything else."

When Josie Smith got in bed she hardly had time to tell Ginger and Percy about her painting because she fell asleep so fast.

★ ★ ★

"Josie! Josie! Wake up and look out of the window!"

Josie Smith jumped out of bed and opened the curtains and blinked at the bright winter light.

"Percy!" she shouted. "Percy! Ginger! Come and see! It's a real snow scene".

She got Percy out from his warm nest in the blankets and took him to sit on the windowsill. Ginger jumped up by himself and yawned and blinked and squeezed his eyes up tight at the bright morning.

It was a real snow scene. Everything was painted in from the blue sky at the top of the black tower to the robin hopping along the top of the wall leaving tiny prints in a line behind him. The brush and bucket in the yard had almost disappeared.

"Ginger," said Josie Smith, "you'd better not go out or else you might disappear. You're not so big." Ginger jumped down and got back in his basket. Percy went back to bed where his nest of blankets was still as warm as toast.

But Josie Smith didn't want to go back to bed. It was Saturday! She got washed and dressed as fast as she could and ran downstairs to the kitchen where she could smell bacon and hot tea.

"Mum, I've got to call for Eileen before everybody else or else I won't get a go on her sledge!"

"Sit down and have your breakfast," said Josie's mum.

Josie Smith sat down. She ate some cereal and hot milk and then some bacon and tomato and toast. She drank some warm milky tea and then she said, "Can I go for Eileen?"

"Put an extra pair of socks on," said Josie's mum, "and bring me your coat, I'll warm it."

Josie Smith brought her old blue coat that was for playing out in and she brought her itchy hat and scarf, as well, to be warmed. "I don't need to warm my gloves," she said. She didn't want her mum to find out that she'd lost one. When she was all wrapped up she went out the front door and made two wellington prints on the doorstep. The bright light made her squeeze her eyes like Ginger as she stamped more wellington prints to Eileen's next door. She rattled the letter box and went in and her heart was going Bam Bam Bam because she was thinking of Eileen's new sledge.

"Is she playing?" Josie Smith asked.

The pretend fire was on and everything was tidy. Eileen was sitting on the flowered carpet in her pink dressing gown, crying.

"I'm not playing out in wellingtons! I'm not! I'm not! *I'm not!*" Eileen screamed and screamed and banged her stockinged feet on the carpet.

"Josie Smith's got *her* wellingtons on," said Eileen's mum. "You can't play in the snow in your best shoes."

Josie Smith waited quietly for Eileen to stop screaming. She only stopped when she got what she wanted and sometimes she didn't even stop then. Josie Smith looked all round the tidy front room. There was no sledge there. Perhaps it was in the kitchen.

Josie Smith said to Eileen's mum, "Please can I have a drink of water?"

"Help yourself," said Eileen's mum. She was struggling with Eileen to try and make her get dressed.

Josie Smith went in the kitchen but she didn't get a glass of water, she just looked.

The sledge was there. It was standing near the door and it was wrapped in a sheet of bright green plastic but Josie Smith could see the metal runners peeping out and a bit of rope and steering bar. The sledge was red and brand new. Josie Smith's chest went Bam Bam Bam. If only Eileen would get dressed so they could set off up to Tag Wood before everybody else came asking for a go.

Josie Smith went back in the front room. Eileen was dressed in her pink anorak with fur round the hood and red wellingtons. She had stopped crying.

"I'm having some real pink snow boots to match my anorak," she said. Then she picked up her doll. "Come on," she said, "We can take our dolls for a walk in the snow."

"Are we not going up to Tag Wood?" asked Josie Smith. "Everybody'll be going sledging."

"We can go if you want," Eileen said, "but I'm not taking my new sledge because everybody'll want a go on it and it'll get all scratched and dirty."

"What's the use of having it then?" said Josie

Smith. "I'll carry it for you, if you want, so you won't have to drag it up the road. It won't get dirty wrapped up in that thick green plastic, I promise it won't."

"You can carry it," Eileen said, "but don't you dare get a scratch on it or I'm telling my mum and you'll have to pay for a new one."

They set off.

A sledge isn't so heavy when you pull it by its rope and slide it along the snow but when you have to carry it, it's very heavy. Josie Smith carried Eileen's sledge round the corner, up the road past Mr Scowcroft's allotment, past her school and the railings behind the playground and up the path to Tag Wood. When they got to the bottom of the slope where everybody was sledging she was puffing and panting. "Aher! Aher! Aher!" Her face was all red and her arms were aching and she was much too hot all over. Her itchy green scarf made her neck terribly hot

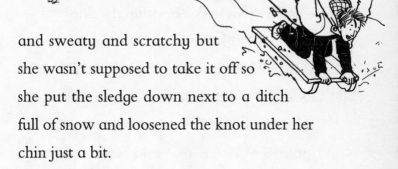

and sweaty and scratchy but
she wasn't supposed to take it off so
she put the sledge down next to a ditch
full of snow and loosened the knot under her
chin just a bit.

Rawley Baxter was sliding down the hill on a
black painted sledge with his coat buttoned
under his chin and flying out behind him.

"Der-der-der-der. Der-der-der-der. Batman!"
He braked with his feet so they didn't fall into
the ditch and snow sprayed all over Eileen.

"I'm telling over you!" shouted Eileen, and Rawley Baxter fired death rays at her and started pulling his sledge back up the slope.

Geoffrey Taylor came down on his sledge and Gary Grimes was hanging on behind him.

"Don't go so fast!" shouted Gary Grimes.

"Don't be so soft!" shouted Geoffrey Taylor and pushed with his feet and went faster and they both fell off. Gary Grimes cried.

Jimmy Earnshaw came down the slope on his old brown sledge. He came down fast but he didn't fall off. He braked near the bottom with his feet and made the snow fly right up in the air. He stopped right at the edge of the ditch.

He saw Josie Smith and said, "Want a go?"

"No," said Josie Smith, "I'm playing with Eileen."

Jimmy Earnshaw pulled a face and started dragging his sledge back up the slope.

"Come on," said Josie Smith to Eileen. "Let's drag your sledge to the top."

"I'm not," Eileen said. "There's loads of rough boys up there and they'll smash my doll. And anyway, I'm not dragging my sledge right up there. It's too heavy."

"I'll drag it, then," said Josie Smith, "and you just carry the plastic. We can sit down on that when we get tired."

"I don't want it," Eileen said. "You keep it. Only, you've got to drag my sledge up as well."

"All right, but you've got to let me have a go on it."

"Go on, then, you can drag it," Eileen said, and they started climbing the slope.

When they got to the top Josie Smith turned the red sledge round and Eileen sat down on it holding her doll.

"If you want to hold the rope and steer you'll have to put your doll inside your coat," said

Josie Smith. "Or do you want me to steer from behind?"

Eileen didn't say anything. She unzipped her pink anorak and put her doll inside it, zipping it up so her doll wouldn't fall out. Then she pushed with her red wellingtons and the sledge started moving.

"Wait," said Josie Smith, "if you don't move up a bit I can't fit on."

"You're not getting on," Eileen said, "only one person has to go on it or it'll break."

"Everybody else goes in twos," said Josie Smith.

"Well, I'm not," said Eileen, "because my sledge is new and I haven't to spoil it."

"Well, you've got to let me have the next go, then," said Josie Smith. "You said I could if I pulled your sledge up the slope. You promised."

"I never," Eileen said. "I only said you could have that green plastic."

"You promised!" shouted Josie Smith. "We played everything you wanted yesterday and today I carried your sledge and pulled it up the slope! You promised!"

"I never said cross my heart and hope to die," Eileen said, and she pushed with her red wellingtons and started going down. She didn't go fast because she was scared. She just kept shunting down a bit with her wellingtons and never let the sledge set off properly.

Josie Smith, holding the green plastic, stood at the top and watched. The slope was shiny with criss-cross lines going all the way down it. At the sides, where the trees were, people were climbing up and pulling their sledges to the top. Then they set off down again.

Eileen, still with her wellingtons planted on the snow, was right in the middle, going as slowly as she could and blocking everybody's way.

"Get out of the road!" yelled Rawley Baxter. "Der-der-der-der. Der-der-der-der. Batman!" Swoosh! He went past Eileen. But Eileen didn't move. She wasn't even going slowly now. She had stopped.

"Get out of the road!" roared Geoffrey Taylor.

"Give her a shove!" shouted Gary Grimes hanging on behind him. Swoosh! They went past Eileen. But Eileen didn't move.

At the top of the slope, holding the piece of green plastic, Josie Smith heard Eileen start to cry.

Two more sledges went past her. Swoosh! Swoosh!

Eileen started to roar.

Josie Smith looked down the slope to where Eileen was stuck. The shiny criss-cross lines that all the sledges had made glinted in the sunlight. They were ice. If you tried to walk down in wellingtons you'd slip.

Eileen roared and roared but Josie Smith didn't know what to do to help her.

Then something went Swoosh and Jimmy Earnshaw set off down on his sledge. When he got just past Eileen he steered his sledge round in front of her so that she wouldn't slide down any further. Then he got hold of her rope and said, "Get on the back of my sledge and I'll take you down."

Eileen got on the back and when he set off,

pulling Eileen's sledge with them, she screamed, "Don't go fast! You haven't to go fast!"

Jimmy Earnshaw didn't go fast. He used his feet for brakes and went down very slowly and stopped before the ditch full of snow at the bottom.

Eileen got off. She grabbed her sledge and ran home crying.

At the top of the slope Josie Smith stood looking down at the criss-cross lines shining in the sunshine. When she had pulled Eileen's sledge to the top she was hot. Now she was cold. She was fed up as well. She wanted to sledge. She didn't want to be a cry baby like Eileen but she wanted Jimmy Earnshaw to rescue her and take her down on his sledge.

Jimmy Earnshaw was taking Ann Lomax down now, going really fast and making her scream and laugh. Next he took Tahara down, going slowly because she'd never been on a sledge before and she was a bit scared. He wouldn't give Josie Smith a ride now because she'd said no when he asked her.

Josie Smith was so fed up she wanted to cry. Her hand with no glove was freezing and aching. She was tired out after carrying Eileen's sledge. She hated Eileen and she hated Jimmy Earnshaw and she even hated the snow.

She was so tired and miserable that she put the stupid piece of green plastic down on the snow and sat on it for a rest, hugging her wellingtons and resting her chin on her knees.

Gary Grimes and Rawley Baxter came up to the top and Rawley Baxter said, "Get out of the road. We want to set off from there. It's the steepest, fastest bit."

"I don't care," said Josie Smith. And Gary Grimes pushed her.

Josie Smith started to say, "Don't you push me, Gary Grimes or I'll... " Then she stopped. Then she said, "Oh! Oh! Aaagh!"

She was off down the slope as fast as lightning. The green plastic slithered down the hard icy snow, lighter and faster than any sledge.

"Help!" shouted Josie Smith.

"Look at that!" yelled Rawley Baxter, and everybody stopped and looked.

"I can't stop!" screamed Josie Smith, whizzing past all the sledges with the wind whistling in her ears.

"Fantastic!" shouted Jimmy Earnshaw. "Look at her go!"

Everybody cheered and shouted.

"I can't stop!" screamed Josie Smith, but everybody was cheering and shouting so hard that nobody heard her.

"I can't stop!" screamed Josie Smith, "I can't stop! I can't... Uffalum."

Uffalum is what you say when you race down a slope on a piece of green plastic and go head first into the ditch at the bottom so that your wellingtons stick up in the air and your mouth fills up with snow.

"Uffalumamoffalum," said Josie Smith as everybody helped to get her out of the ditch and she tried to get the snow out of her mouth and then her ears and then her hat and then her wellingtons.

"You look like a snowman," Gary Grimes said.

"With a red nose like a carrot," Rawley Baxter said.

Jimmy Earnshaw brushed some snow off the back of her coat and said, "Can I have a go on that plastic?" And Josie Smith let him.

Everybody wanted a go but then a lot of people dashed home and came back with cut up laundry bags and big rubbish bags. Jimmy Earnshaw came back with a post sack because his dad was a postman. The last go they had they knotted all the pieces of plastic together in a long line and they all whizzed down the hill side-by-side and fell into the ditch with their wellingtons in the air. Uffalum!

Then Gary Grimes said, "I'm starving!" And everybody else felt hungry too so they folded up their plastic sheets and ran home for their dinner.

"Mum!" shouted Josie Smith, crashing in at the front door, "Mum! We played sledging and we all went down together and everybody fell in the ditch! And, Mum…!"

"Good heavens," said Josie's mum.

"Good heavens," said Josie's gran who had come for her dinner.

"You look like a snowman," said Josie's mum. "Take those wellingtons off."

She had to take her socks off as well because there were lumps of snow and ice stuck all over them. She stood there on the rug in her snowy coat and bare red feet and creases in her forehead because she was worried.

She was worried because her mum was holding her green anorak and out of the pocket she took one brown glove.

"Well?" said Josie's mum. "Where's the other one? Have you lost it?"

Josie Smith shut her eyes.

"Now, Josie," said Josie's gran, "you tell the truth like a good girl."

Josie Smith's chest went Bam Bam Bam and she didn't dare open her eyes because she daren't tell the truth.

"Well?" said Josie's mum. "I won't ask you again. Where's your other glove?"

Josie Smith, holding her breath and keeping her eyes shut tight, pretended to look for her glove in her pocket. Then her eyes opened wide and out of the pocket she pulled a glove!

"No wonder you can never find them," said Josie's mum, "if you keep one in your blue coat pocket and one in your anorak. Now, when that one's dry, roll them up together and put them in the top drawer."

"And while you're waiting for it to dry," said Josie's gran, "try these."

And she gave Josie Smith a pair of soft warm mittens with stripes of all the colours of the rainbow *and* a bobble hat and scarf to match.

"D'you know what?" said Josie Smith with a

big smile. "Everybody'll be able to see me if I'm painted in a snow scene. And, d'you know something else? I'm never ever ever going to lose these gloves!"

And, believe it or not, she didn't.

Order Form

To order direct from the publishers, just make a list of the titles you want and fill in the form below:

Name ....

Address ....

....

....

Send to: Dept 6, HarperCollins Publishers Ltd, Westerhill Road, Bishopbriggs, Glasgow G64 2QT.

Please enclose a cheque or postal order to the value of the cover price, plus:

UK & BFPO: Add £1.00 for the first book, and 25p per copy for each additional book ordered.

Overseas and Eire: Add £2.95 service charge. Books will be sent by surface mail but quotes for airmail despatch will be given on request.

A 24-hour telephone ordering service is available to holders of Visa, MasterCard, Amex or Switch cards on 0141- 772 2281.

Collins
An *imprint of* HarperCollins*Publishers*